Dear Parent:

Remember the first time you read a book by yourself? I do. I still remember the thrill of reading the words Little Bear said to Mother Bear: "I have a new space helmet. I am going to the moon."

Later when my daughter was learning to read, her favorite I Can Read books were the funny ones—Danny playing with the dinosaur he met at the museum and Amelia Bedelia dressing the chicken. And now as a new teacher, she has joined the thousands of teachers who use I Can Read books in the classroom.

I'm delighted to share this commemorative edition with you. This special volume includes the origin stories and early sketches of many beloved I Can Read characters.

Here's to the next sixty years—and to all those beginning readers who are about to embark on a lifetime of discovery that starts with the magical words ***"I can read!"***

Kate M. Jackson

Senior VP, Associate Publisher, Editor-in-Chief

I Can Read!™ BEGINNING 1 READING

Sammy THE SEAL

story and pictures by SYD HOFF

HARPER
An Imprint of HarperCollins*Publishers*

I Can Read Book® is a trademark of HarperCollins Publishers.

Library of Congress Cataloging-in-Publication Data

Hoff, Syd, date

Sammy the seal / story and pictures by Syd Hoff.

p. cm.—(An I can read book)

Summary: Anxious to see what life is like outside the zoo, Sammy the seal explores the city, goes to school, and plays with the children but decides that there really is no place like home.

ISBN 978-0-06-257274-5

[1. Seals (Animals)—Fiction. 2. Zoos—Fiction. 3. Humorous stories.] I. Title. II. Series.

PZ7.H627Sam 2000 99-13805

[E]—dc21 CIP

AC

16 17 18 19 20 SCP 10 9 8 7 6 5 4 3 2 1 ❖ Originally published in 1959

Sammy THE SEAL

It was feeding time at the zoo.
All the animals
were getting their food.

The lions ate their meat.

The elephants ate their hay.

The monkeys ate their bananas.

The bears ate their honey.

Then it was time
for the seals to be fed.
Mr. Johnson took them fish.

“Hooray for fish!” said the seals.

They jumped in the water.

Soon the basket was empty.

“That is all there is,” said Mr. Johnson.

“There is no more.”

“Thank you for the fish,” said the seals.

“They were good.”

The seals were happy.

But one little seal was not happy.

He sat by himself.

He looked sad.

"What is wrong, Sammy?"

said Mr. Johnson.

“I want to know

what it is like

outside the zoo,” said the little seal.

“I want to go out and look around.”

“All right, Sammy,” said Mr. Johnson.
“You have been a good seal.
You may go out and see.”

“Good-bye, Sammy,” said the other seals.

“Have a good time.”

“Good-bye,” said Sammy.

“Where are you going?” said the zebra.

“I am going out,” said Sammy.

"Have fun," said the hippo.

“Come back soon,” said the giraffe.

Sammy walked and walked and walked.

He did not know what to look at first.

“That seal must be from out of town,”
said a man.

Sammy looked at everything.

"What street is this?" said a man.

"I am a stranger here myself,"

said Sammy.

"I guess it is feeding time here, too," said Sammy.

“That is a lovely fur coat,” said a lady.
“Where did you get it?”
“I was born with it,” said Sammy.

“I wish I could find some water.
I am hot. I want to go swimming,”
said Sammy.

“We are sorry. There is no room for you in this puddle,” said the birds.

"And there is no room for you here," said the goldfish.

“Keep out,” said the policeman.

“You cannot swim in there.”

“Ah, here is a place!” said Sammy.

"Who is in my bathtub?" said someone.

"I am sorry," said Sammy.

He left at once.

Some children were standing in line.
Sammy got in line, too.
"What are we waiting for?"
asked Sammy.

"School. What do you think?" said a boy.

"That will be fun.

I will come, too," Sammy said.

The teacher was not looking.

Sammy sat down.

The children made words with blocks.

Sammy wished he could spell.

"All right, children.
Now we will all sing a song,"
said the teacher.

The children had good voices.

“That sounds fine,” said the teacher.
“But one of you is barking—
just like a seal.”

"Is it you, Joey?"

said the teacher.

"No," said Joey.

"Is it you, Helen?"
said the teacher.
"No," said Helen.

"Is it you, Dorothy, Robert,
Fred, Joan, or Agnes?"
"No," said the children.

"Then it must be you,"

said the teacher.

“I am sorry. This school is
just for boys and girls.”

“Please let me stay,” said Sammy.

“I will be good.”

“All right. You may stay,”

said the teacher.

Sammy was happy.
He sat at his desk
and looked at the teacher.

He learned how to read.

He learned how to write.

"And now it is time to play,"

said the teacher.

"Who wants to play a game?"

"We do," said the children.

They threw the ball over the net.

"The ball must not hit the ground,"
cried Sammy's team.
"Somebody catch the ball."

Sammy caught the ball on his nose!

A boy on the other team tried
to catch the ball on his nose, too.
"Boys must catch with their hands,"
said the teacher.

Sammy tried to catch the ball
with his flippers.
"Seals must catch with their noses,"
said the teacher.

Up and down went the ball,
from one side to the other.
At last the teacher blew her whistle.
"Who wins?" said the children.
"It is even," said the teacher.
Everybody was happy.

A bell rang. School was over.
“Will you be here tomorrow?”
said the children.
“No,” said Sammy.
“School is fun,
but I belong in the zoo.
I just wanted to know
what it is like outside.
Now I have to go back.”

“Good-bye, Sammy,” said the children.

“We will come to see you.”

“Good,” said Sammy.

Sammy was in a hurry
to get back to the zoo.
He had so much to tell the other seals.

“May I welcome you home, Sammy,”

said Mr. Johnson.

“I am glad you are back.

You are just in time for dinner.”

"There's no place like home,"

said Sammy.

"I can read! I can read! Where are the books for me?"

One question from a young reader sparked a reading revolution!

A conversation between the director of Harper's Department of Books for Boys and Girls, Ursula Nordstrom, and Boston Public Library's Virginia Haviland inspired the I Can Read book series. Haviland told Nordstrom that a young boy had burst into the children's reading room and asked her where he could find books that were just right for a brand-new reader like himself.

Determined to fill this gap, Nordstrom published *Little Bear* by Else Holmelund Minarik, with illustrations by Maurice Sendak, in the fall of 1957. The response was immediate. According to the *New York Times*, "One look at the illustrations and children will grab for it. A second look at the short, easy sentences, the repetition of words, and the beautiful type spacing, and children will know they can read it themselves."

Delightful and wonderfully warm, *Little Bear* served as the template for the series, and now, sixty years later, we have over four hundred I Can Read stories for our youngest and newest readers!

Where the Ideas for the Characters Came From

Berenstain Bears

Stan and Jan Berenstain were cartoonists in the 1950s. When their sons began to read, they submitted a story about a family of bears to author, editor, and publisher Ted Geisel (aka Dr. Seuss), which was published as *The Big Honey Hunt* in 1962. Geisel labeled their next effort "Another Adventure of the Berenstain Bears." That's how the bears got their name!

Biscuit

One day while watching her daughter play with their neighbor's frisky dog, Alyssa Capucilli was struck by her daughter's patience and gentle nature, as well as the fact that her little girl thought the dog understood every word she said. That was the inspiration for the little yellow puppy and his sweet companion. Pat Schories's warm illustrations capture their tender relationship.

Pete the Cat

When James Dean first saw Pete, he was a tiny black kitten in a shelter. Pete looked like he had been starved and his black fur was a mess. At first, James had no interest in Pete—black cats were bad luck, after all! But the scrawny little fellow stuck his paw out of the cage, wanting to play! James took Pete home. And even though James chose to paint Pete the Cat blue (his favorite color), James realizes now that black cats are actually very good luck.

Danny and the Dinosaur

In 1958, cartoonist Syd Hoff's daughter Susan was going through a rough surgery, and one day, Syd decided to draw a picture to cheer her up. It showed a dinosaur with Syd's brother on its back. When Susie saw the picture, she exclaimed, "Danny and the dinosaur!" and that night after the family went to bed, Syd wrote the story.

Pinkalicious

Victoria Kann's daughters could never seem to get enough of cupcakes or the color pink! One year, as an April Fools' joke, Victoria told her family and friends that one of her daughters had turned pink from eating too many pink cupcakes—and so the idea for *Pinkalicious* was born!

Frog and Toad

The characters of Frog and his best friend, Toad, might have been inspired by . . . a horror movie! Arnold Lobel and his daughter, Adrianne, went to see a movie called *Frogs* at the drive-in. However, the movie featured not frogs, but toads! Adrianne told her dad about the many differences between the two—and two years later the first Frog and Toad book, *Frog and Toad Are Friends*, appeared.

Little Critter

Mercer Mayer was doodling around one day in 1974 when he drew a shape like a gourd, put two eyes on it, scribbled a nose connecting the eyes, then got coffee and forgot about it! The next day, he noticed a small piece of paper on the floor. It was his gourd. He added fuzzy hair and a big mouth; short stubby arms and feet. Mercer had created a fuzzy little "woodchuck-y porcupine" thing that became Little Critter!

Fancy Nancy

When Jane O'Connor was a small girl, every Sunday, when her grandma and great aunts came to visit, Jane would greet them at the door in a tutu and a pair of her mom's high heels. She thought she looked très glamorous!

Years later, while she was fixing dinner one night, the name Fancy Nancy flew into Jane's head, and a star made her debut!

Amelia Bedelia

Amelia Bedelia was inspired by Peggy Parish's third-grade students at the Dalton School in New York City. The children mixed up words, and Parish found them hilarious. That gave Parish the idea for Amelia Bedelia—a character who takes every word literally and embraces life with an outlook that is forthright and optimistic. Illustrator Fritz Siebel worked with Parish to create the perfect look for the conscientious cleaning lady.

Early Character Development

The Berenstain Bears

Stan and Jan Berenstain's early sketches from *The Berenstain Bears Clean House*

Pete the Cat

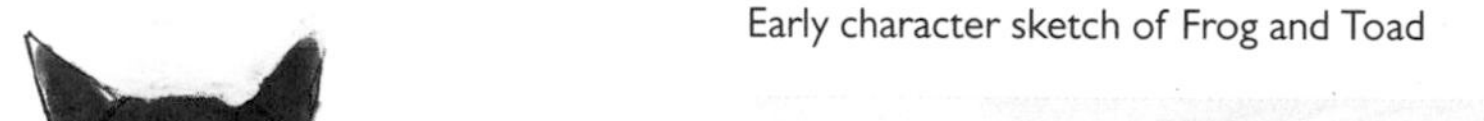

James Dean's first painting of Pete the Cat

Frog and Toad

Early character sketch of Frog and Toad

Biscuit

Biscuit character sketches

Pat Schories's early sketches from *Biscuit*

Pinkalicious

Victoria Kann's sketches for the picture book *Pinkalicious*

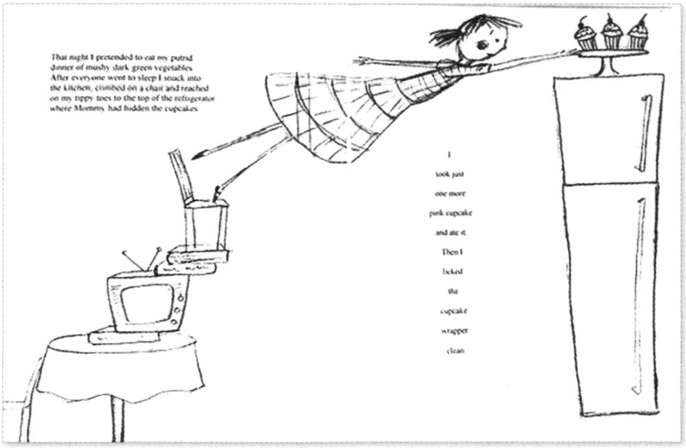

Amelia Bedelia

Fritz Siebel's sketches for the picture book *Amelia Bedelia*

Danny and the Dinosaur

Syd Hoff's early cover sketches for *Danny and the Dinosaur*

Little Critter

Mercer Mayer's early character sketches of Little Critter

Fancy Nancy

Robin Preiss Glasser's character sketches and cover sketch for *Fancy Nancy and the Boy from Paris*

These two catalogs marked the launch of I Can Read!

Sixty Years of I CAN READ

1957
Little Bear

1958
Danny and the Dinosaur

1959
Sammy the Seal

Emmett's Pig

1960
Cat and Dog

1961
*Little Bear's Visit**

1963
Amelia Bedelia

1970
*Frog and Toad Are Friends**

A Bargain for Frances

1972
*Frog and Toad Together***

1984
In a Dark, Dark Room and Other Scary Stories

1986
The Josefina Story Quilt

1996
Biscuit

2005
The Berenstain Bears Clean House

2008
Fancy Nancy and the Boy from Paris

Little Critter: Snowball Soup

2010
Pinkalicious: School Rules!

2013
Pete the Cat: Pete's Big Lunch

2017
Long, Tall Lincoln

* Caldecott Honor titles
** Newbery Honor